MW00531921

Pomegranate Portland, Oregon

Published by Pomegranate Communications, Inc.
19018 NE Portal Way, Portland OR 97230
800 227 1428 | www.pomegranate.com

Pomegranate Europe Ltd.
Unit 1, Heathcote Business Centre, Hurlbutt Road
Warwick, Warwickshire CV34 6TD, UK
[+44] 0 1926 430111 | sales@pomeurope.co.uk

To learn about new releases and special offers from Pomegranate, please visit www.pomegranate.com and sign up for our e-mail newsletter. For all other queries, see "Contact Us" on our home page.

Library of Congress Cataloging-in-Publication Data

Jones, DuPre.
The adventures of Gremlin / by DuPre Jones ; drawings by Edward Gorey.
pages cm
ISBN 978-0-7649-6605-7 (alk. paper)
1. Fairy tales--Humor. I. Gorey, Edward, 1925–2000, illustrator. II. Title.
PS3560.O48A3 2013
813'.54--dc23

2013004982

Pomegranate Catalog No. A221

Designed by Lynn Bell, Monroe Street Studios

Printed in China

22 21 20 19 18 17 16 15 14 13 10 9 8 7 6 5 4 3 2 1

Chapters

1. The Wombat

In the kingdom of Etaoin there once lived a little boy and girl named (respectively) Zeppelin and Gremlin. Zeppelin was Gremlin's brother, and Gremlin was Zeppelin's sister. They were very unhappy children, for they dwelt all alone in a small cottage in a great forest. They had a father, but he was a woodsman who was usually away in another part of the forest felling trees. As for their mother, she had long ago deserted the family to become a seamstress in the camp of a local bandit and philanthropist named Robin Hood. Her name was Little John.

Zeppelin and Gremlin had very little to eat except rutabagas and kumquats, which grew abundantly about the cottage. As for playmates, there were only the woodland animals, but most of these were burrowing marsupials. Theirs was a very dreary life, you may be sure.

One day, however, the children had a very interesting experience. They were tripping through the forest—the children tended to trip and stub their toes, for they had

no shoes—munching rutabagas, when Gremlin espied a most curious thing.

"Look!" she whispered, gripping Zeppelin's emaciated forearm.

There before them, swinging a lighted lantern in one tiny paw and in the other a tinkling bell, was a wombat.

As the boy and girl stared in amazement, the creature proceeded to enact a wondrous ritual. He would scamper around a tree, swinging his lantern and bell to and fro; every few minutes he would pause, stare into the upper branches of the tree, and cock an ear as if expecting some kind of message. Throughout all of this activity the wombat murmured to himself such strange words as *"de mortuis nil nisi bonum," "morituri te salutamus,"* and *"magnae spes altera Romae."*

After watching this astonishing demonstration for quite some time, Gremlin could withhold her curiosity no longer, and approached the furry fellow.

"Excuse me for bothering you, Mr. Wombat," she said.

The wombat stopped circling the tree and looked at her. "Yes," he said peevishly, "what is it?"

"I know it's none of my business," said the little girl, "but I should certainly like to know why you run around the tree as you do, and say funny words, and look up at the top of the tree as if there were something there."

"Hell," said the wombat, "it's a living."

2. The Singular Parrot

Zeppelin and Gremlin were more than a little bewildered by their encounter with the wombat. Even so, what they had seen and heard had made a tremendous impression on them. If such awesome things could occur right on their very doorstep, think of the exciting magical experiences that must lie beyond! So the children decided to set off to explore the world that very day.

In no time at all—after packing a basket of goodies (minced rutabagas and candied kumquats) and leaving a farewell note to their papa—they were on their way.

Elated with dreams of new lands and new adventures, the little boy and girl skipped along merrily, pausing to gasp in amazement at exotic birds and beasts—denizens of the strange new wonderland.

At the sight of one of these, Gremlin gave a cry of pity. It was a bird, flapping its heavy wings to rise, but returning to earth after each brief flight.

"Are you hurt?" asked Gremlin. "Can I help you?"

"Kakapo," answered the bird. "Kakapo."

Gremlin gave a cry of pity.

"I beg your pardon?" said Gremlin. "Er, *nicht sprecht. Ne parle pas.*"

"Kakapo," the bird repeated. "That's me. *Strigops habroptilus.* A singular parrot. Although I have well-developed wings, I can fly but little. Or so it says in Webster's."

"Gee, that's too bad," said Zeppelin. "Do you feel bad, not being—one of the birds, as it were?"

The kakapo shrugged. *"Non omnia possumus omnes."*

"I'm glad we've met you, anyway," said Gremlin. "You see, we're off to see the world, and we would appreciate any advice you could give us on where we ought to go."

"Well, I don't get around much, of course," said the kakapo, "but by keeping my ear to the ground I've gotten a pretty good idea of the lay of the land. All Etaoin is divided into three parts. Over there," he said, pointing his well-developed wing to a path on the left, "is the Enchanted Forest part. I don't know that I'd recommend it. From what I've heard it's rather a weird area. Everyone who goes in there comes out as a toad or a snake—that sort of thing. The rest stay there as loathly ladies or trees. (Fradubio was a very bad case, very bad.) Anyway, if you two are the kind of young people who think it's necessary to go around sopping up experience, that's the Enchanted Forest."

"What are the other parts of the kingdom like?" said Zeppelin excitedly.

The kakapo motioned with his beak. "That middle path leads to the sea. I hear it's pretty there," he said wistfully, "but lately it's been overrun with pirates and brigands and other riffraff."

"The world seems like an awfully dangerous place," observed Gremlin.

"That's what they tell me," the bird answered wryly. "Now, the last path, over there to the right, will take you to the Imperial Palace, where the King and Queen live."

"Oh," said Gremlin, "what are they like?"

"They're all right. Big Divine Righters—you know, absolute monarchists, and powerful, but a lot of dissent in the kingdom."

"It's all so thrilling," exclaimed Gremlin, "that I think I want to see it all."

"Me too," shouted Zeppelin. "Let's go to the Enchanted Forest and work East."

They turned down the left-hand path. "Good-by, Mr. Kakapo. Thanks for your help, and for foreshadowing the plot."

"Don't mention it," said the bird as they disappeared down the path. "Keep out of trees."

3. The Candy House

As Zeppelin and Gremlin skipped merrily down the path to the Enchanted Forest, their insouciance soon gave way to trepidation, although they would not let themselves admit it—and certainly not in those words. The woods grew dark and whispery; the air became filled with the cries of owls and rusty grackles; the path narrowed; branches reached out to clutch the now-terrified children. It was fearsome.

Suddenly, however, the children turned into a clearing, where they stopped short, unable to believe their eyes. Before them stood by far the more extraordinary of the two houses they had ever seen. A jelly-bean walk led to licorice steps. The walls were pralined. The doors were éclaired. The very shingles on the roof were of Nestle's Crunch.

Throwing aside their lunch basket, Zeppelin and Gremlin literally ate up the ground to the front door, which they also ate. It was not until they had eaten the front porch and half the living room that they became aware that someone was staring at them. It was a witch—and with her malevolent toothless grin and burning eyes, obviously a wicked one.

As if to allay any doubts on that score, the witch began to shriek, dance about, and beat the earth with her broom. "Eeeeeee," said the witch. "I'm the wickedest witch there is."

"What do you do that makes you so wicked?" asked Gremlin, feeling nauseated.

"Are you kidding?" said the witch. "I eat little children. Cannibalism and infanticide in one gobble. Can you imagine anything more disgusting?"

"No," admitted Gremlin.

"Now," said the witch, "I'm going to boil you in oil and gobble you up, just as you gobbled up my beautiful house," whereupon she seized the frightened children and bound them with a stout cord.

The witch then commenced brewing a rank-smelling fluid in a huge cauldron, stirring it with an ivory ladle, muttering incantations (e.g., "Rows disarrayed; violences blue; seraglios weep; and so will you"), and performing an evil dance, much of it indecent.

When the proper mixture was cooked and the proper spell evoked, the wicked witch untied the boy and girl and prepared to toss them into the boiling vat. But just at this moment a ravenous bear thundered out of the forest, grabbed the wicked witch and Zeppelin, and ate them. Gremlin took this opportunity to hide in a clump of hydrangea, where she lay panting for breath and feeling simply dreadful.

When the bear had finished its meal, it spied Gremlin quivering in the bushes and lurched over to look at her.

"Oh, please, Mr. Bear," said Gremlin, "don't eat me. I'm just a little girl out to see the world, and I've run into all sorts of terrible difficulties."

"Don't worry, little girl," said the bear. "I'm not going to eat you. The fact is I've had too much already. You might say," he added apologetically, "my eyes were bigger than my stomach."

"I know just how you feel," said Gremlin, "but all the same, I wish you hadn't eaten my little brother, for now I haven't anybody to see the world with."

"Oh, I am sorry," said the bear. "But as Housman said,

> 'The grizzly bear is huge and wild;
> He has devoured the infant child.
> The infant child is not aware
> It has been eaten by the bear.'"

"I suppose so," said Gremlin despondently.

"I must go now," said the bear. "I'm glad for your sake I'm not hungry anymore."

"So am I," said Gremlin, and fell into a deep sleep.

4. The Fairy Godmother

When Gremlin awoke she was startled to see standing over her a beautiful lady who emanated radiance for some eight or nine inches in all directions.

"Why, you must be my fairy godmother," cried Gremlin.

"Correct," said the fairy godmother. "Hey, kid, you wanta look at some funny photographs?"

"I don't feel much like it now," said Gremlin. "You see, I've had the most awful . . ."

"How about a nice cigarette? Make you feel funny."

"No, thank you, I don't smoke," said Gremlin. "Besides . . ."

"Mescaline? LSD?"

"Well, I am a little hungry," said Gremlin.

The fairy godmother sighed. "Never mind, honey. Now, what can I do for you? As you doubtless know, I am, as your fairy godmother, entitled to grant you three wishes."

"I didn't know that," exclaimed Gremlin. "How exciting!"

"You wanta look at some funny photographs?"

"First off," cautioned the fairy godmother, "let's get the rules straight: none of this hanky-panky about wishing for an indefinite number of wishes. My union—the International Godmotherhood of Fairies—strictly forbids it. We'd be working around the clock."

"Oh, three seems a very generous number to me," said Gremlin.

"Another thing," said the fairy godmother. "If I hear just one more time the joke that goes 'Make me an ice-cream soda; poof, you're an ice-cream soda,' I'm quitting the whole business. Just be a good girl and ask for a prince or something."

"Could I have my brother back?" asked Gremlin.

"Nothing to it," replied the beautiful lady, thrice waving her magic wand in a circle. Immediately Zeppelin appeared, looking a little bewildered but otherwise none the worse for wear or bear. Gremlin gave a cry of delight and ran up to embrace her brother.

"Hello, Zep," she said. "How do you feel?"

"A little peaked," admitted Zeppelin. "I don't think it's so much from the bear eating me as from my eating that living-room wall. There's probably a moral there."

"You mean, there's probably a mural there," suggested the fairy godmother.

Zeppelin winced.

"Nobody likes my puns," said the lady sadly.

"It's not that," said Zeppelin. "I'm just not feeling very well." Actually, he was trying not to hurt the feelings of his rather belated *deus ex machina.*

"You have two more wishes," the fairy godmother reminded Gremlin. "What'll you have?"

Gremlin thought about this for a while. "To tell you the truth, I can't think of anything just now. May I save the wishes and use them later?"

"Sure," said the fairy godmother. "Whenever you want me, all you have to do is say the magic words 'Mafficking Malachi'; then I'll appear and grant your wish. Now, if you don't need me anymore, I'll disappear."

"All right," said Gremlin. "We'll be continuing our adventures now. We plan to go to the sea, where we've been told all sorts of interesting things happen."

"Yes," said the fairy godmother, "the beach is nice this time of year. But, for heaven's sake, try to stay out of trouble. And don't feed the bears."

"Good-by, fairy godmother."

"Good-by," said the luminous lady, vanishing.

5. The Sylvan Bard

Zeppelin and Gremlin had gone quite some distance through the forest without encountering any adventures when, rounding a curve in the path, they stumbled over a pair of outstretched legs and went sprawling. Looking up, they discovered that the legs belonged to a young man with long golden hair who was sitting with his back to a tree, scribbling energetically on a notepad.

"Excuse us," said Gremlin. "We didn't see you there."

"Excuse *me,*" replied the young man. "I'll be with you in a moment, but first I must put the finishing touches to one of my most transcendent verses."

"Oh, are you a poet?" asked Gremlin.

"Ah, yes," answered the youth with a dreamy smile, at last taking his eyes from the paper to regard the children. "Ah, yes."

"We'd love to hear some of your poems," Gremlin said, "if you wouldn't mind reading them."

"Splendid," cried the poet. "I'm so pleased that you have asked me. Out here in the wilds"—he gestured—

"one forgets that one is, after all, communicating—mystically perhaps—with the very fibers of other souls (I am tempted to say Everysoul, or, perhaps, Allsoul, as there is a bit of Everyman in every man), and not with the narcissistic mirror of genius."

Zeppelin and Gremlin sat down before him with a simulated expression of hushed expectation.

"Since my work is considered in some obtuse circles as 'obscure,'" the poet went on, smiling bitterly at the word 'obscure,' "you will not object to a brief prefatory explanation to each of my readings?"

"Num um," murmured the children diffidently.

"This piece," the young man said, turning to a page of his tablet, "seemingly a work of senseless brutality, is in reality an exposé of this era of violent decadence in which we live. It also demonstrates the need for a reactivated feminist movement, and is, as you will note, thoroughly oriented in Freudian symbolism." He cleared his throat.

> "There once was a man from Algiers
> Who grabbed a young girl by the ears;
> He shook her and shook her,
> Till wrath overtook her,
> And she cut off his necktie with shears."

The poet beamed as Zeppelin and Gremlin applauded politely.

"My next poem prophesies the eventual doom of the *bourgeoisie,* and demonstrates urban depravity at its worst:

"There once was a man from Astoria
Who shattered his spouse's euphoria:
'Our daughter,' he said,
'Has been shot through the head,
While frequenting sordid emporia.'

"And this one," he continued excitedly, no longer taking any heed of the children, "once and for all refutes the Andocresalian metaphysic:

"There was a young mystic from Libya
Who said, 'This is true, I won't rib 'ya:
I was walking to heaven
With some friends (there were seven),
When Jupiter fell on my tibia.'"

Turning to the next page, the poet assumed a stern visage. "Here," he said, "is a powerful protest against vivisectionists, to whom I am strongly opposed:

"There once was a man from Verdun
Whose idea of rollicking fun
Was to take wings from flies—
And their legs, and their eyes—
Then throw them on people and run.

'While frequenting sordid emporia.'

"Next," began the poet, but Gremlin interrupted.

"Your poems are wonderful, but if we're going to explore the world, we really can't stay any longer."

"Oh, just a quickie," said the poet impatiently. "This next opus tells of a miraculous vision I had during the recent eclipse:

"A mariner bound for Good Hope
Found a shrimp at the end of a rope.
    Or was it the hemp
    At the end of the shrimp?
Is the question worth pondering? Nope.

"Now," he continued feverishly, "a graphic tribute to the vegetarian persuasion:

"A curious diner named Irving
Asked the waiter just what he was serving.
    He replied, 'It's a dish
    That is truly delish,
But the contents are simply unnerving.'"

"We really must . . ."

"Wait, wait!" cried the poet. "A rhyme explaining the mysteries of the Mass:

"'The devil you say,' said the priest
To the baker, 'We never use yeast

In our bread. It will rise
With our Lord in the skies
(Our sav-i-our, lately deceased.)'"

Zeppelin and Gremlin rose. "We're sorry," said Zeppelin, "but we really must be off now."

"Oh, all right," said the young man dejectedly, "but how about one for the road? It's all about the language barrier."

"All right," said Gremlin, "if you promise it's the last."

"Hrrrumph," began the poet:

"A girl named Hélène from Dry Butte,
When asked for her name grew quite mute.
'The problem,' she said,
Sadly shaking her head,
'Is not only grave, it's acute.'"

At this moment a giant, who had been lurking behind a nearby redwood tree, leaped out, picked up Zeppelin and Gremlin in either hand, and went crashing through the forest with them.

"Help," screamed Gremlin to the young poet, "do something!"

"I'm sorry," responded he, "but I'm afraid I'm quite powerless against giants. But you may rest assured I will compose a splendid elegy for you."

Zeppelin peered at him over the thumb of the huge hand that held him. "When you do," he yelled in an unwonted spirit of acerbity, "try rhyming 'intellectual' with 'ineffectual.'"

The giant and his little prisoners disappeared into the forest.

6. The Giant

It is very uncomfortable to be carried along in the fist of a giant, especially if his palms perspire.

"Say, giant," hollered Gremlin, "where are you taking us?"

The giant made no reply.

Gremlin repeated the question, then again, then a fourth time, then a fifth.

Finally the giant perked up the ear nearest Gremlin and brought the little girl close to its giant pink shell.

"Where are you taking us?" said Gremlin loudly.

"Well," answered the giant malevolently, "it isn't to a land flowing with milk and honey, honey. By the way," he added petulantly, "you don't have to shout."

"What will you do with us?" asked Gremlin more softly. "Eat us?"

The giant shuddered. "What a revolting thought! What do you think I am, anyway, a monster? No, I've more utilitarian designs for you. I'll put you in bondage,

I expect, and work you until you're old and haggard. Heh," he snickered, "ain't that mean?"

"We're too little to be of any use," pleaded the little girl. "Why didn't you take the poet instead? He could compose lovely sonnets and couplets and things for you."

"Nah," said the giant. "I got no use for literature. Unschooled, that's me. I guess that's why I turned out to be such a brute. Anyway, as for you, don't worry. I'll think of something to keep you weary and miserable."

Gremlin began to cry. "Oh," she moaned, "and we were going to have such wonderful adventures."

"Whaddaya mean," roared the giant. "It isn't every day you get picked up by a guy forty-eight feet tall. At your age," he said, squinting at Gremlin, "it isn't every day you get picked up."

"But," Gremlin wept, "now we'll have to stay prisoners forever and ever."

"Aw, it won't be so bad," consoled the giant. "I got lots of other helpless little boys and girls locked up. Give you a chance to meet some slaveys your own age."

"Boohoo," said Gremlin.

"Will you stop that infernal yawling!" demanded the giant, banging his fist against a hillock. "Ooops," he said.

"Now," bawled Gremlin, "you've gone and squashed my brother."

The giant shrugged. "'Life,'" he said, "'like a dome of many colored glass' only 'stains the white radiance of eternity' anyway."

"I think you're misreading that," said Gremlin.

"Maybe so," said the giant. "Like I said, I never been a great one for literature." He deposited Zeppelin atop a tall tree, and they continued on their way.

By and by Gremlin and the giant came to a castle which was so huge that, to Gremlin, it looked like heaven itself. At this thought, another thought—a horrifying one—occurred to Gremlin.

"Are you God?" she yelled up at her captor.

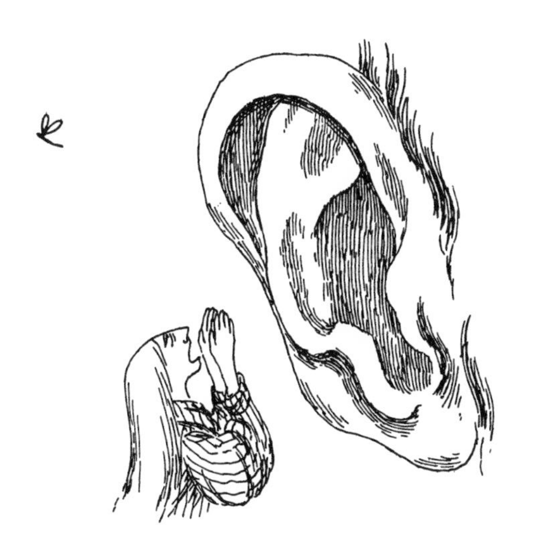

"What's that?" roared the giant, again drawing the little girl close to his cavernous ear.

"Are you God?" repeated Gremlin.

"Oh, no," said the giant, with a laugh as loud as creation. "Whatever gave you that idea? My name is Umlaut, and I'm pretty satanic most of the time."

"Well, I must say I'm relieved that you're not God," Gremlin said. "If this were heaven we're coming to, I would have liked to think I could enter it at my own free will."

"That's a very interesting concept you've just brought up," replied Umlaut, "but theology is a little out of my line, too. In fact, I'm not good for much of anything except being a nasty brute. And I'm extremely competent at it, too," he added modestly. "'A small thing, but mine own.'"

"Perhaps you'd like trying to be good for a change," suggested Gremlin. "Get a girlfriend. I'm sure many a nasty brute has been reformed by the love of a good giantess."

"No," Umlaut sighed. "Although I do have a way with women: I disgust them. Besides, what you can't seem to understand is that I love being terrible. I love to torment, torture, destroy, and corrupt. Come along, now," he said, striding into the castle, "and I'll show you just what I mean."

7. The Dungeon

Umlaut's first act of wanton cruelty to Gremlin was to throw her into a dungeon filthy, cramped, and crowded with dozens of ragged, starving, beaten, miserable children. Gremlin stared aghast at the squalor of her prison.

The other inmates seemed barely interested in the new arrival, but Gremlin—as was her nature—decided to go about making friends right off.

"How do you do," she said to the dungeon-at-large. "My name is Gremlin, and I hope that despite the hopelessness of our situation we can all be good friends and begin to make plans to escape this terrible place in which we find ourselves entrapped at such a tender age."

A wretched little girl spoke up. "You can lay off the Y.W.C.A. gambit," she said. "That won't go over here. As for the escape bit, forget it. You remember the last children's crusade. We have about as much chance of getting out of here as a Popsicle in an oven."

"I hate to see you all so disheartened," said Gremlin.

"'So much a long communion,'" answered the little girl, "'tends to make us what we are.' *The Prisoner of Chillon.*"

"Yes," replied Gremlin, "'. . . you and I who've spent so many pleasant years together. 'Tis sorry work to lose your company / Who clove to me so close.' Cosmo Monkhouse: *Any Soul to Any Body.* Still, it seems as though we ought to try."

"It's no use," reiterated the little girl. "Our only chance is that the only man in the world of whom the giant is afraid will come to rescue us. That's the Red Cross Knight (who has a certificate in life saving). But he's always so busy pricking across the plain, he hardly ever has time for liberating little people anymore. No, Gremlin-or-whatever-your-name-is, 'Faiths by which my comrades stand / Seem fantasies to me, / And mirage-mists their Shining Land, / Is a strange destiny.' Hardy."

"Well, let's get acquainted, anyway," said Gremlin. "What's your name?"

"We all go by the names of the maladies we've contracted here," the little girl said. "My name is Scrofula. And over here"—she pointed to a group of youngsters huddled against the wall—"are Beriberi, Trenchmouth, Scurvy, and Iron Deficiency Anemia."

"I'm pleased to meet you all," smiled Gremlin, curtseying.

"Pleestameecha," chorused the children.

"As for getting out of here," said Gremlin, "there is really nothing to it. You see, I have a fairy godmother, and all I have to do is say the magic words for her to appear and grant my wishes."

"Sure," said Scrofula, "and I'm Cinderella and these other kids are the Seven Dwarfs and the Three

Bears." Those among the children who could laugh did so cynically.

"Just you wait and see," replied the unperturbed Gremlin. "I'll say the magic words now and a beautiful lady will appear from out of nowhere and have us out of here in a jiffy."

"Okay, sweetie," said the little boy named Trenchmouth, "show us your stuff."

But as Gremlin opened her mouth to summon her fairy godmother, she was horrified to realize she had forgotten the magic words.

"Menacing mayhem," she ventured cautiously.

Nothing happened.

"Malpracticing medicos," she tried; then, in rapid succession, "tremulous truffles," "languishing liederkranz," and "suffering succotash."

"I'll think of it in a minute," said Gremlin, becoming a little flustered.

"Sure you will," said Scurvy. "Just you let us know."

She didn't, though, and despite several more imaginative alliterative attempts, nothing at all resembling a miracle occurred. The only result of all Gremlin's activity, in fact, was that the other children began addressing her as "Stircrazy."

8. The Rescue

Two years passed. Life in Umlaut's castle was just as dismal and hopeless as the giant had promised. The children were up from morning to night at the cruel, back-breaking tasks the giant assigned them, and casualties were high among the inmates. The giant—it is only fair to record—gave these unfortunates proper burial, even to the extent of inscribing traditional (if garbled) epitaphs on their little tombstones (e.g., "He is not sleepeth, but dead.")

Of course, there were sporadic and desultory attempts to escape by the more adventurous of the children. The incentive for breaking out, however, was discouraged greatly by the fact that attempts were always discovered and the culprits punished in a manner quite severe—even for Umlaut! Boys and girls caught trying to escape were used as badminton birds in games played with visiting giants. Few children were known to survive a sustained volley.

Despite the confinement and hard work, Gremlin—to the astonishment of her fellow prisoners—

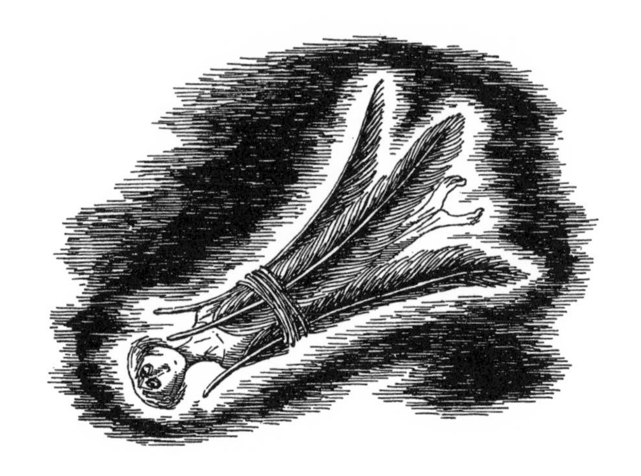

maintained her youthful energy and rosy complexion. This, she modestly explained to the others, was her reward for faith and clean living.

Try as she might, Gremlin could not remember the magic words which would summon her fairy godmother, but she was certain that one day she would. Then she would not only liberate the children but resuscitate Zeppelin and continue her adventures with him.

In the end, though, it was not the fairy godmother who came to the rescue of the children, but the Red

Cross Knight, whom Scrofula had mentioned upon Gremlin's arrival.

He came charging up to the castle one day at full tilt astride his white steed, magnificently arrayed in golden armor.

"What ho!" yelled the Red Cross Knight.

"Not much," roared the giant from his battlements. "What ho with you?"

"I have come to challenge you to combat," answered the knight. "I've heard you're running a white slavey racket, and I have been commissioned by the king to put a stop to it forthwith."

"You and who else?" Umlaut yelled back, throwing open the castle gates and striding forth.

"Me and right, decency, valor, continence, honor, chastity, humility, and our Heavenly Father, that's who," retorted the knight sharply.

The battle that ensued is too complicated to describe with a great deal of accuracy, and too gory to detail with the necessary verisimilitude. The giant was powerful but clumsy. What proved Umlaut's undoing was his rather unwise decision to wear sandals in combat. He was felled finally by a series of nicks and scratches around his feet and ankles, inflicted by the lance of the Red Cross Knight as he circled and dodged on his skilled charger. Shouting at the top of his lungs and hopping around on one foot and then the other, Umlaut was brought down—with a tremendous thud—by a swift sure jab in the second toe of the left foot.

Immediately the Red Cross Knight scrambled onto his huge opponent's chest and pointed his sword at his throat.

"Yield," demanded the gallant knight, "or I will chop off your head."

"Have you any idea how long it would take you to chop off my head?" said the giant. "Days. But your point, as it were, is well taken. I yield. Uncle."

The children who had been watching the combat through the tiny dungeon window let out a well-meaning but feeble "Huzzah."

"Now you must free those unfortunate wretches and let them return to their homes," commanded the Red Cross Knight sternly.

"Okay," said Umlaut. "I know when I'm licked."

The children were set free in no time, and stood blinking in the unaccustomed sunlight before departing for their homes.

There was no small number of tearful farewells, and even some vague talk of a kind of class reunion in ten years, but the children were soon on their ways, eager for mother, dad, and hearth.

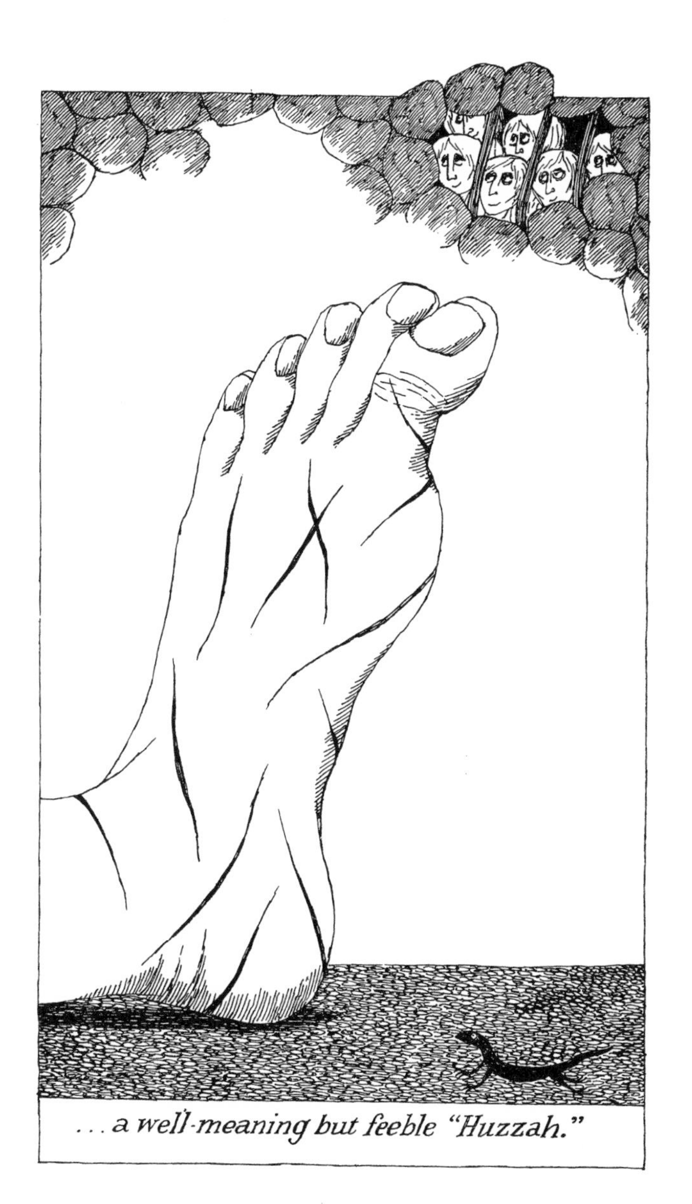

. . . a well-meaning but feeble "Huzzah."

"So long, Stircrazy," said Scrofula to Gremlin, waving as she trudged wearily off. "If you ever run into that fairy godmother of yours, have her make me an ice-cream soda."

As most of the children moved away, Gremlin began to feel very lonely and sad. She certainly did not want to return to her home, nor did she wish to continue her adventures without her brother, who was dead to the world unless she could remember the magic phrase. A solitary tear ran down her brave little cheek.

Noticing this, the Red Cross Knight approached Gremlin and laid a compassionate hand on her head.

"What's the matter, little one?"

So Gremlin told the Red Cross Knight her whole story, which the good man found most astonishing.

"Never you mind," he assured her. "I'll take you along with me on my search for the Holy Grail, and meanwhile—heh, heh—maybe we'll find your fairy godmother. My name is Red Cross Knight, but you can call me Red. By the way," he added, lifting her into the saddle, "do you mind if I call you Stircrazy?"

9. The Vision

Gremlin found life with the Red Cross Knight exciting and eventful. There was always a dragon to slay, a distressed damsel to rescue, or some wrong or another to avenge. Gremlin would sit on the sidelines, cheering wildly and applauding as the knight went about his dedicated duties with efficient gallantry.

There was also the matter of the Holy Grail to discover, but Gremlin soon wearied of the quest. The Red Cross Knight, being virtuous, honest, steadfast, loyal, brave, and true, was also trusting and credulous. He was easy prey for every drummer and con man in the kingdom. Each time he made inquiry about the Relic, someone would be there to step up and whisper in his ear: "Holy Grail, eh? Yessir, I got the Real McCoy right here." And each time he was gulled. Proudly fondling his purchase, the Red Cross Knight would soon discover a telltale piece of evidence to reveal he had been betrayed: "Made in Japan"; or "T. C. Quimby and Sons, Toronto"; or "Bangkok World's Fair, 1644."

In four years of questing, the Knight had accumulated three hundred and forty-six flagons and chalices of various shapes and sizes, plus enough pieces of the True Cross to erect a good-sized house.

But the Red Cross Knight never lost his sanguine nature or simple faith, however many setbacks he suffered. Certainly, he was the very essence of kindness and courtesy to Gremlin.

The girl knew well enough that virtue is its own reward, but she began to wonder why so good a man as the Red Cross Knight, who spent all his time questing and doing good and being chivalrous, shouldn't get a little thanks now and then for all his trouble. So she asked him.

"I'm glad you asked me that," answered the Red Cross Knight. "I don't know."

"Then I'll tell you," came a melodious voice from behind them. Turning around, Gremlin and the knight were flabbergasted to see—encircled in light and sitting on a fluffy pink cloud—an angel, who flashed a pretty white smile at them and raised a hand in beatific greeting.

"I'm an angel," she said by way of introduction.

"Yes, we can see that," said Gremlin reverently.

"I overheard your conversation a moment ago," continued the angel, "so I thought I'd float down and drop in a word or two of encouragement."

"The Good Shepherd looks after his own," she said, assuming a more solemn tone, "and I want you to know you've already been separated from the goats in His book. But if you want to attain a prize as valuable as the Holy Grail, you will have to do more than kill off a few dragons and rescue maidens and little girls. Any gentleman would do as much. No, you must meet a far greater challenge. You must overcome"—she paused dramatically—"the Seven Deadly Sins and the Seven Lively Succubi."

The Red Cross Knight thought about this for a moment. "In that order?" he said finally.

"Yes," replied the angel firmly.

"I mean," the knight went on, "I couldn't take on the Seven Lively Succubi and *then* the Seven Deadly Sins?"

"No," said the angel. "Now, I've told you the arrangements. Pass this test and your quest will be ended."

"Thank you so much," said the Red Cross Knight. "It kind of gives me something to go on."

"Hope you make it," said the angel. "Good-by and good luck." And with that she was gone in a flash.

10. Three Sins

"That's a pretty tall order," said Gremlin to the knight as the angel disappeared into the heavens. "Do you think you're up to it?"

"I guess we'll just have to wait and see," said the Red Cross Knight. "But it does seem like a pretty hard row to hoe."

They didn't have to wait long for the first temptation. Wrath, in the form of a little green pixie with a two-pronged pitchfork, was sitting on a rock around the very next bend in the road.

"Hello, Cubscout," the pixie greeted the knight. "My name is Peter Pain. Your mother was a trollop and your father was a communist."

"Now, that simply isn't true," replied the knight reasonably. "My father was landed gentry—a capitalist in fact—and my mother was a great lady. They were hardly . . ."

"Ah, go __________ __________," said Peter Pain nastily.

"That," answered the knight, "is not only immoral but impossible."

"Your brothers were panderers and your sisters took dope," sneered the pixie.

"Wrong again," said the Red Cross Knight, smiling easily.

"Guess you're the wrong ______ ______," said the temptor, getting off the rock to come closer. "I've got it," he said, eyeing the knight's armor, "you're the tin woodman and this little ______ ______ ______ ______ is Dorothy."

"No," answered the Red Cross Knight patiently, "this little lady is named Gremlin, or Stircrazy, and I'm . . ."

Peter Pain banged the pitchfork down on top of his helmet so hard that the whole suit of armor vibrated.

"Bet that smarts," said Peter Pain.

"That it does," said Red. "You pack quite a wallop, little fellow."

"Okay, ______ ______, you've passed the first test," said Peter Pain. "Now, beat it."

"You were wonderful," the little girl said admiringly as they rode away. "I would have been furious."

"It was nothing," the Red Cross Knight replied modestly, smiling through clenched teeth. "In fact, I'd enjoy meeting that ______ ______ ______ ______ little fellow again someday."

The road to Envy was clearly marked farther down the road by a sign which read: This Way To The Super DeLuxe Modern Demonstrator Home.

"Ooo, let's go see," said Gremlin, and so they did.

Winding its way through a beautiful garden was a walkway studded with emeralds and rubies and pearls. Gremlin could hardly contain herself. "Isn't it simply gorgeous?" she cried to her friend.

"I suppose so," said the knight indifferently, "but don't you find it a bit, er, *de trop?*"

The house was made of the finest marble, except for the door and window frames, which were silver, and the roof, which was platinum.

Gremlin and Red were greeted at the door by an obese man wearing nylon Bermuda shorts, a tattersall vest, a houndstooth jacket, and a vermilion tie with a hula girl painted on it and, in luminous chartreuse, the letters M-O-T-H-E-R.

"How do you like it?" said the fat man, indicating the house. "Just bought it the other day as a summer place. Plan to spend a week or two here every year. Boy, I sure bet you wish you had it, huh?"

Red shrugged.

"However could you afford such a scrumptious place?" Gremlin asked.

"Don't you find it a bit, er, de trop?*"*

"Ah, this is nothing," the man replied. "You ought to see the place back home. I made it all on some crooked real estate deals last year. People call me a dirty bourgeois and *nouveau riche* and all that, but what the heck? Beats pricking across the plain for a living, eh, knight?"

"Splendor opum sordes vitae non abluit umquam," replied the knight. "Come, Gremlin, let us be off."

"Like a little loot to take with you?" asked the rich man as they left.

"No," said Red, "we never take handouts."

"I sort of wish you had accepted a little money," Gremlin said. "I sure am getting hungry."

"Poor child," said Red. "We'll stop at the next eatery."

This proved to be an establishment which advertised itself by means of a big neon sign as

NIKOS' BUFFET DINER
ALL YOU CAN EAT FOR FOUR DANDIPRATS
WELCOME GLUTTONS

"That certainly seems reasonable," Red said, studying the sign. "Let's go in."

They were met inside by a smiling Greek waiter. "Please to come een," he said, bowing. "Four dandiprat' an' he'p yousevs."

On a huge table which lined three sides of the wall was a feast fit not for a king, but a god. Every imaginable variety (and a few more) of meat, fish, fowl, vegetable, and dessert was there, all prepared with the finest Hellenic culinary touch. Gremlin, who had hardly eaten anything for two days, scampered excitedly here and there, heaping her plate with squab, venison, lobster, and seven varieties of pastry. Only after she had sat down at a table and begun filling her empty little belly did she notice that the Red Cross Knight, after carefully surveying the rich table, had put only a chicken leg and a bagel on his plate.

"Eat up, Red," said Gremlin through a mouthful of pineapple upside-down cake. "At least put down that old drumstick and get a piece of the breast."

"The dark," said the knight, seating himself beside her, "is light enough."

Soon the meal was finished, and the two were on their way again.

"That certainly was a wonderful dinner," said Gremlin happily.

"It was adequate," said the knight. His stomach growled. "Excuse me."

11. Four Sins

Gremlin had to admit that Red had handled the temptations of wrath, envy, and gluttony with consummate control. She was a little ashamed that she had herself succumbed so easily to each of these temptations.

The next challenge was one which Gremlin was a little too young to understand.

They were riding along beside a little adobe hut when a young lady in a peasant blouse (what there was of it) leaned out of a window.

"Hiya, snooks," said the young lady to Red, "whatcha doin' . . . way out here in the country . . . all by your lonesome?"

"As you can see, mademoiselle," said the knight, "I have a companion."

"Hello, Miss," said Gremlin.

"You don't look like a cradle-robber, handsome," the woman answered. "How 'bout a little powwow with a real woman for a change? Like . . . now."

"Like . . . now."

Red squirmed in his saddle. "Well," he said to Gremlin. "I guess I can't very well handle the temptation way down here."

"What temptation?" said Gremlin.

"Never mind," said Red. "Just you wait here." And with that, he dismounted his steed and strode boldly into the hut.

In a moment he was back.

"What happened?" asked Gremlin.

"Certes, nothing," said Red, smiling through clenched teeth. "She remained more chaste than kind. Never laid a glove on her. Four down and three to go."

As they rode along, Gremlin overheard the knight muttering to himself something like, "a man's reach should exceed his grasp, or what's a heaven for?"

The fates, as if amazed by the knight's continence, tried for a tricky double play on avarice and sloth.

Red and Gremlin had been riding for two days without rest, and were very nearly spent, when they came to a real dilemma. On one side of the road stood a quiet, homey little inn, and on the other was a pile of debris. In front of each was a little old lady.

"Hello," chorused the ladies. "We've been waiting for you."

"Indeed?" said Red. "Whatever for?"

“I’m here,” said the old lady in front of the inn, “to offer you free lodging for the night and a soft, downy bed to take your rest.”

“While I,” said the other old lady, “am asking you to erect from this rubble a dwelling just as tidy and neat as my neighbor’s across the way. For this service I will pay you fifty million dandiprats, which is far, far more than the job is worth and will put you on Easy Street for the rest of your life.”

“So if you accept my offer,” said the first, “you will be guilty of laziness.”

“And if you accept mine,” said the other, “you will be guilty of greed.”

“And if I do neither?” asked the Red Cross Knight. “If I simply ride on down the road and resist the temptations of both sloth and avarice?”

The two old ladies looked at one another. “Golly,” they said, “we didn’t think of that.”

“Then I bid you farewell, ladies,” said Red, and off he and Gremlin went down the road.

As they rode along, Red began to snicker, then chuckle, then chortle. Finally he stopped his horse and practically fell to the ground, convulsed with laughter.

“Did you see the expressions on their faces?” he roared at Gremlin. “Oh, did I ever outsmart those old harpies. Wow, am I *smart!* I mean, am I clever or am I clever? Yessir, you've got to get up pretty early in the morning to put one over on old Red Cross Knight."

At this point, Red became aware that someone other than Gremlin was regarding his amusement, and sternly. It was the angel, sitting on her little cloud.

Something dawned on the Red Cross Knight.

"Oops," he said.

"Hubris and hamartia," intoned the angel solemnly, *"hubris and hamartia."*

"You tricked me," said Red. "Anybody would have been proud to have outwitted that ruse. You just can't win."

"And now you shall not be allowed to discover the Holy Grail," said the angel sadly. "And you seemed like such a promising boy."

"How about the seven lively succubi?" asked Red. "I guess that's out, too?"

"Yes," said the angel, "you've failed."

The Red Cross Knight thought for a moment, then brightened. "Well," he said, "since I've failed, there's no great harm, is there, in my going back for a somewhat longer and more fruitful visit with that little thing at the hacienda?"

"I guess not," said the angel.

Red brightened further. "Or picking up some easy dough on that construction job?"

"No."

"Or really tieing on the feedbag at that Greek restaurant?"

"No."

"Or going back and kicking the _______ out of that little green _______?"

"No."

"Well, angel," said Red, with not very convincing *doleur,* "I'm sorry it didn't work out, but as they say, 'many are called but few are chosen.'"

"That's about it," said the angel.

"Now I've got some traveling to do," said the Red Cross Knight, reining his horse about.

"Red Cross Knight," said Gremlin, "what about me?"

"Kid," said the knight affectionately, "it's been swell, but I'm afraid things are going to be a little different from now on. Come see me when you're a little older."

"Good-by, Red," Gremlin said.

"Good-by, Stircrazy."

And he was gone.

Gremlin turned to the angel and knelt before her. "Lady of the heavens," she cried, "will you help me?"

"Who do you think I am," said the angel, disappearing, "your fairy godmother?"

12. The Saracen

Gremlin was a plucky little girl, so—lonely and abandoned as she was—she immediately began planning what to do with herself in this predicament. She decided that traveling through the enchanted sector of the kingdom had been, as a whole, less than salutary, and that she must at all costs get out of it and into a different sort of territory. Behind her there were, among other things, a bear and a giant to contend with. Ahead of her lay the terrible kingdom of Shrdlu, ruled over by a tyrannical gnome king named Grig. The western boundary, it was said, marked the end of the world. To the east was the dangerous seashore. Anywhere one went, it seemed, there were difficulties. But Gremlin decided that the eastern route was best, because it led ultimately to the safety of the Royal City.

The immediate problem was to ascertain which direction was east. The only way to find out, obviously, was to ask someone. So Gremlin sat down under a shady tree to await a passerby.

By-and-by along came a knight, dressed from head to foot in black. This struck Gremlin as singular and more than a little foreboding, but she hallooed the knight just the same.

The black knight rode up, got off his horse, and looked at Gremlin.

"Good afternoon," said the little girl. "My name is Gremlin. What's yours?"

"Mine is Tsome Nkome," replied the knight. "I'm a Saracen, which means I'm one of the bad guys, although that's really a relative position depending on which side one is on. I can't help it if I'm a paynim."

"I suppose not," said Gremlin. "I knew a Christian knight, but he turned out rather badly."

"Red Cross Knight?"

"Why, yes," said Gremlin. "Do you know him?"

"Sure," the Saracen said. "Why, I challenged him up the road not an hour ago, but he was in a tearing hurry. Said he was too busy."

"I know," sighed Gremlin.

The Saracen peered at her for a moment. Then he said, "My dear, I have bad news for you. I am going to have to take you prisoner."

"Indeed?" asked Gremlin. "Wherefore?"

"Don't play coy with me," replied the knight, chucking her playfully under the chin, "and you the king's daughter."

"You are very mistaken, sirrah," cried Gremlin. "I am the daughter of a homely woodcutter, and I have never so much as laid eyes on the king."

"No," said the Saracen, scrutinizing her again, "you're the goods all right, the rightful heiress to the throne of Etaoin."

"How can you tell?" queried the puzzled little girl.

"You might say that your age, the mole on your right earlobe, the birthmark on your left elbow, and the fact that one of your eyes is blue and the other green gave me a couple or three hints."

"Well, if I'm the king's daughter," Gremlin demanded, "what am I doing in this neck of the woods?"

"It's a long story," said the paynim patiently. "All I know is that you had a jealous aunt with aspirations to the throne. Right after you were born she set you adrift in the bulrushes in a little boat. No one's heard of your whereabouts since."

"So I'm the princess," exclaimed Gremlin. "Wow!"

"But I'm afraid I'll have to take you captive now," said the knight reluctantly. "You're worth a king's ransom. Will you come peaceable, or do I have to tie you up?"

Gremlin went along, peaceably, to the Saracen's hideout, which turned out to be a deep cave at the foot of a mountain. Therein, the black knight chained her to a stalactite and told her to be patient until he returned from posting the ransom note. He informed her that sandwiches, soft drinks, books, and magazines were within chain's length, and told her just to make herself at home.

"Good-by," said Gremlin. "Hurry back."

13. The Escape

Gremlin made herself a raspberry jam and salmon sandwich and sat back to munch on it while she surveyed her prison. On the wall was a shotgun (out of Gremlin's reach, unfortunately) with the strange word Tchekhov scrawled underneath the mounting. There were also a number of brazen images and oriental bric-a-brac, and a small shelf of books.

One of the latter caught Gremlin's attention: *Mediaeval Ballads, Tales, Oaths, Union Songs, Calls for Help, Magic Spells, and Phrases by which to Summon Faerie God-Mothers,* edited by F. J. Childs. Grosset and Dunlap. 1514.

Gremlin excitedly seized the book and turned to the phrases by which to summon fairy godmothers, which she began reading aloud, one by one. There were thousands, of course, and by the time she reached "Mafficking Malachi"—which Gremlin recognized immediately—she was so hoarse that she was afraid she wouldn't be heard.

It worked, however. Once again Gremlin's fairy godmother stood before her.

"Hello, dearie," she said. "Long time no see." She squinted around the dim cave, her gaze pausing on the shotgun. Finally her eyes came to rest on the chain which bound Gremlin to the stalactite. "It's no wonder," she said, "that you wanted to get in touch with me."

"I would have done so sooner," Gremlin said, "because I've been in and out of some terrible scrapes. But I couldn't remember the magic words until I saw them in this book. Now could you bring Zeppelin back so he can set me free?"

"Again?" said the fairy godmother. "You've sure got an unlucky brother."

"Except that he isn't really my brother. I'm actually the king's daughter, you see."

"How long have you been here?" said the fairy godmother. "You sound a little stircrazy."

"No," said Gremlin, "I really am princess of Etaoin. And Zep has been so close to me it would be unthinkable not to have him share in the good of my returned fortune. So, will you bring him here unsquashed?"

The fairy godmother waved her wand and there was Zeppelin!

"You sure took your time about it."

"You sure took your time about it," were his first words. "What happened?"

"Never mind that now," said Gremlin. "We have to get out of here before the Saracen comes back. Find some way to remove this chain."

"Okay," said Zeppelin. "I don't know what a Saracen is, but I'm willing to bet it's one of the bad guys."

"So long, kids," said the fairy godmother, beginning to vanish. "Remember you've only one wish left."

"I will," said Gremlin. "Thanks again."

Zeppelin meanwhile had begun rummaging through the Saracen's tool chest, where he soon found just the instrument he was looking for: a pneumatic hacksaw. In a very short time—though it seemed an eternity—Gremlin was free, and off she and Zeppelin went as fast as they could go.

When they were a safe distance from the cave, they stopped, panting for breath. Gremlin then told Zeppelin all about the adventures she had had while he was "away." Zeppelin found them all most thrilling, especially the part about Gremlin's being a princess.

"Before Mother left home," he said, "Father used to refer to 'that cock-and-bull story about finding Gremlin in the bulrushes.' I never knew what he meant till now."

The Saracen returned to his cave a short time later, looked wistfully about, sighed, and stared ruefully at the shotgun.

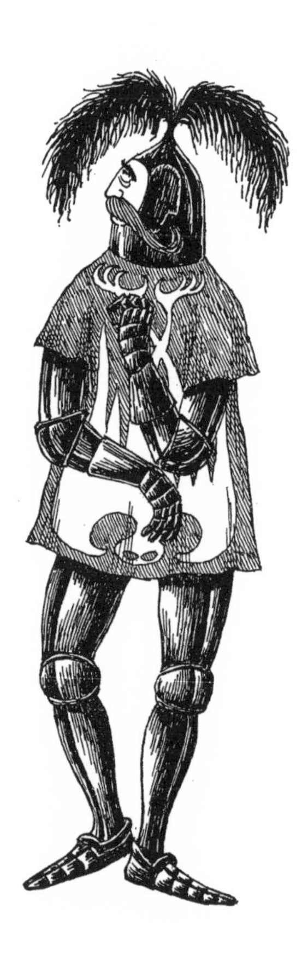

14. The Inn

Zeppelin had the good sense to note that if the sun went down in the west, then the east must lie in the opposite direction. So, early next morning, rested and refreshed, Gremlin and her foster brother were headed out of the enchanted forest and into whatever new adventures might await them.

"I wish we had brought along some food from the Saracen's cave," Gremlin complained. "I certainly am hungry."

"So am I," said Zeppelin, "but maybe we'll find somebody soon who will share a little something. Look," he said, pointing down the road, "I think there's an inn."

Gremlin saw a small building just ahead with a swinging sign in front which read Ye Old Coffee Shoppe. "Goody," said she. "Let's go in. Although we haven't any money, perhaps they will let us work for a meal."

Inside the inn it was so dark that for a moment Zeppelin and Gremlin couldn't see a thing. When their eyes finally became accustomed to the gloom, they could just make out a few tables occupied by a number of men in beards and navy pea jackets, and girls with long straight hair and navy pea jackets. There was also a table with coffee-making apparatus on it, and a small bandstand upon which four musicians (lute, lyre, recorder, and tympani) were performing.

The boy and girl approached a man behind the counter.

"Excuse me," began Zeppelin, "but we were wondering if we might work for . . ."

"Work?" said the man. "No, man. No work here."

"But we're trying to get some food," Gremlin protested.

"Food?" said the man. "Like you got espresso, you got a baroque combo, who needs it?"

"Never mind," said Zeppelin. "I sure don't understand this place," he added to Gremlin.

"Neither do I," said she. "Everyone is so quiet and sad-looking. Let's ask someone why this is so."

They walked over to a table where a particularly morose-looking couple was sitting.

"What's the matter?" asked Gremlin kindly. "Has something happened?"

"Has something happened?" repeated the bearded man. "Has something happened? Like it does not swing any more, like Lostville, like Deserted Village. Like you

was the afterbirth of man in a pot. Like the sad lousy howl of the ai had flown the eucalyptus tree. Like the ree-bopbop of a tin song on the juke:

> Yessir, that's my baby,
> Her elbows are crisped and sere,

She buys her clothes at Gerfendoerfer's:
Undies in the rear.

Shall I compare thee to a jar?
Masticate your gum.
Publish glad tidings of fratricide,
My King Kong kingdom come.

Like there was none but the lonely flick house, the phony coney, the lollapalooza. Like the bird had flown with his horn. Like what you gonna do when it all runs dry? Like drown? Like go down like into a whirlpool with the dead jellyfish? Like a little bug spray on the anthill, maybe rock 'em sock 'em dead, like a little orange juice in the gutter. Like a fat man creoled in a chimney; God, where do impala live? Like go sell it on the mountain. Like beer on a mahogany bar, like elbows all soggy, like the foam gets all tangled in your beard. Like how are you fixed for blades? Would you, could you be a tedious elysium some other way? Like a dirty old man on a superhighway, get up, move, like before a greyhound runs over your feet."

"Solid," said the girl sitting next to him.

"I still don't understand," Zeppelin said. "Let's go find someplace where we can get some food."

15. The Berry Patch

Zeppelin and Gremlin hadn't gone much farther on their journey before they came to an orchard, full of the most delectable-looking fruits and berries. They fell to with a will, particularly on a bush of delicious orange-colored berries.

As they ate, a funny thing happened. The berries kept getting harder to reach, and bigger. It was some time before they realized that it wasn't that the berries had gotten bigger but that they, Zeppelin and Gremlin, had gotten smaller. In fact, when they had stopped gorging themselves and took time to try to get a perspective, they had shrunk to a height of about three inches each.

"Mercy," cried Gremlin, "what have we done?"

"You've eaten a bunch of shrinkaberries, that's all," piped a tiny voice.

"Who said that?" said Zeppelin, looking around.

"I did," said a little girl—also three inches high—emerging from behind a leaf.

"Why, you're tiny, too," observed Gremlin.

"I also ate some of those orange-colored berries," explained the girl. "Shortens the hell out of one, as you can see."

"But this is terrible," Gremlin exclaimed. "What shall we do?"

"That's simple, too," answered the mite. "Just eat some expandaberries. Those are the purple ones over there. They'll make you big again in no time."

"Well, if that's true," said Zeppelin, "why haven't you done it?"

"Oh, I got to where I like it this way," answered the little girl. "In my quiet way, I'm quite distinctive."

"But if all we have to do is eat the purple berries to get big again," argued Zeppelin, "what's the point of this episode? It isn't even exciting."

"Don't speak too soon," said the little girl, ducking back behind the leaf. "There come some giant hedgehogs."

Sure enough, thundering down upon them were two giant hedgehogs. They weren't really giant hedgehogs. They were normal-sized hedgehogs, but speaking relatively, that is, from a point of view three inches off the ground, they were big enough to scare the wits out of Zeppelin and Gremlin.

"Come on," said Zeppelin, grabbing Gremlin's arm and racing for the purple berry tree, "we've got to get big again."

They each seized a purple berry and began munching on it furiously. Just as the hedgehogs got to them, Zeppelin and Gremlin shot up to their normal sizes.

"Whew," breathed Zeppelin, "that was a close one. Sorry, hedgehogs," he said, looking down.

"Not so fast," shouted one of the hedgehogs. "Four can play that game." And with that the hedgehogs seized *two* purple berries apiece and popped them into their mouths. A moment later they really were giant hedgehogs.

"Grrr," said the second hedgehog. "Now we gotcha."

Zeppelin and Gremlin, of course, retaliated by eating more berries until they were again larger than the threatening beasts. This went on for some time, each opponent outgrowing the other, until the first hedgehog said, "Whoa. Let's start eating the orange berries and outshrink each other, just for a change."

"Why don't we forget the whole thing?" suggested Zeppelin. "It's a stalemate, any way you look at it, and there are any number of ways to look at it."

"All right," said the second hedgehog, "agreed."

Pretty soon Zeppelin and Gremlin were back to their normal sizes and bade *adieu* to the hedgehogs, who were back to theirs.

"Good-by," said the first hedgehog. "Vertical chases are fun. We'll have to do it again sometime."

"I think not," said Zeppelin. "Good-by."

To Gremlin he said, "I still think the whole episode was pointless," and she said, *"C'est la vie."*

Nevertheless, after this Zeppelin and Gremlin were sure to be very careful what they ate, and this should be a valuable lesson for all little boys and girls.

16. The Pirates

The sea, which Zeppelin and Gremlin reached after another two days' travel, was the most beautiful sight they had ever beheld.

"All those buoys and gulls," cried Zeppelin. "I can't get over it."

The excited children spent many happy hours playing on the beach, making sand castles, wading in the surf, and doing all the things children at the beach normally do. They had three-legged races and built human pyramids (the first pointless and the second difficult, when only two are involved). But soon it was time to move on.

They hadn't gone far when Zeppelin cried out, "A boon! A boon!"

"What's a boon?" Gremlin inquired.

"It must be some kind of rowboat," said the boy, "because there's one now."

Sure enough, a little skiff was bobbing at the water's edge.

"Now we shan't have to walk anymore," Zeppelin went on, "and by continuing our journey by water we can avoid those brigands the kakapo told us about."

Alas, Zeppelin's ideas about travel proved wiser in theory than in fact. For no sooner had they boarded the little dinghy and pulled anchor than they were swept up in the current. The children's furious paddling proved utterly useless against the force of the sea.

"Oh," wailed Gremlin, "now we shall be swept out to sea, and after all our fabulous adventures I shall never be able to see my parents, the king and queen, and take my rightful place upon the throne of Etaoin."

"That's a nice recap," said Zeppelin, "but I think we are saved. There's a big ship up ahead, and if we row just as hard as we can I think we can reach it."

Reach it they did, but after they had clambered up on deck for a look around, they were almost ready to throw themselves once again upon the mercies of the sea. For this was a pirate vessel, bearing the name *Il Hombre Dangereux* and flying the Jolly Roger.

For the moment, the children's arrival on board had gone undetected, for the crew were all occupied at the other side of the deck in a cruel and frightening sport. Spurred on by their villainous-looking peg-legged captain, the men were throwing ballast stones at a surprised flock of sea birds who were resting just off the starboard side.

"Kill! Kill! Kill!" screamed the captain in a frenzy of sadism. "Leave no tern unstoned."

When the men were exhausted and the surviving birds had flown away, the captain turned and noticed Zeppelin and Gremlin standing diffidently on the deck.

"Blubber my guts!" he screamed. "Landlubbers! Avast there!"

"Hello, captain," lustily yelled Zeppelin, who had always been told to greet the obscene with a cheer. "Are you fellows pirates?"

"Well," said the captain, momentarily dropping his blustery demeanor, "we like to call ourselves privateers. We're known around the seven seas," he said almost shyly, "as the finny tribe. It's a neo-classical conceit."

He resumed his rough manner. "But we've no place on this ship for children. Why, rumbriny, I'll just have to throw you overboard, that's what."

"You can't do that," Gremlin said in an incipiently queenly tone, "for I am princess of the land."

The captain stumped over to look at her more closely. "By thunder," he thundered, "so you are. Way I can tell is . . ."

"I know," Gremlin said. "By the mole on my right earlobe, the birthmark on my left elbow, and my duochromatic eyes."

"It's a neo-classical conceit."

"Right, your highness," said the captain, bowing. "My name is Longjohn Slivers. And now . . ."

"I know," Gremlin said. "You're going to hold me captive, for I must be worth a king's ransom."

"Salt my kippers, little lady, but you know all the answers. Yessir, you're worth a hundred million dandiprats if you're worth a sou. Seize her," he ordered two of his men, "and take her below."

They did.

Longjohn cast a glittery eye on Zeppelin. "As for you, my lad, it's walk the plank."

"But, sir," said the quick-thinking lad, "surely you could use a good cabin boy."

"Blast my golliwogs!" hollered the captain. "I could use a boy to clean up some of the mess around here, at that." He lowered his voice and again abandoned his swaggering manner. "The crew," he whispered to Zeppelin, "being the scum of the earth, are less than couth in their sanitary habits.

"Now get to work," he shouted, "before I keelhaul ye."

"Yes, sir, captain, sir," said Zeppelin, "and thank you."

17. The Whale

It cannot be said that Gremlin and Zeppelin enjoyed their maiden voyage at sea. Zeppelin was forced to work all day scrubbing decks, filling tankards with rum, throwing slops over the side, and doing any number of menial tasks. But at least he had the run of the ship, while Gremlin—although much better treated because of her station—was confined all day to her cabin with nothing to amuse her but battered copies of such books as *The Yachting Almanac* and *Tom Swift and His Atomic Submarine.*

One day, Zeppelin—whose young ears were privy to many a salty conversation among the crew—overheard a bit of information so disturbing that he could hardly wait until the hour when he was allowed to visit Gremlin to tell her of it.

"Grem," he said to her at once, "we've been duped, doublecrossed, and shanghaied."

"Don't worry," said Gremlin. "When daddy comes through with the ransom . . ."

"That's just it," Zeppelin interrupted. "I heard two of the mates talking. When Longjohn Slivers gets the money—which, incidentally, will just about bankrupt the kingdom of Etaoin—he intends to keep it and then deliver you to Grig, the king of Shrdlu, as a political hostage. It all spells doom for your country."

"Gramercy," said Gremlin, "this means I shall have to summon my fairy godmother to extricate us from this dilemma. I had so hoped to save my last wish for an emergency."

"'Sblood," said Zeppelin. "That's too bad."

But before Gremlin could even utter the magic words, a tremendous thud shook the three-master from stem to stern. It was as if the ship had been hit by a whale—which in fact it had. Pandemonium broke loose above and below decks. The ship was filled with the sounds of splintering timbers, falling masts, running feet, and repeated panicked cries of "The White Whale! The White Whale!"

Zeppelin and Gremlin ran topside amid the general confusion. Everywhere they looked men were abandoning the vessel, which was obviously sinking.

"I hate to desert a sinking ship," said Zeppelin, "but, after all, we didn't ask to come here. We'd better make a jump for it."

They ran to the vessel's stern and prepared to leap, when they suddenly drew back in terror. There, staring

directly at them, was the enormous baleful eye of the whale!

"Oh, please, Mr. Whale," shouted Gremlin, "please don't swallow us when we jump ship, which we have to do, you see, because you've broken it all to pieces."

"Yes," boomed the whale, smiling his wide smile, "I really smashed it up, didn't I? But what's all this about swallowing you? What are you, anyway, fundamentalists? You're certainly not pirates."

"No, we're just children who were captured by privateers while we were making a perfectly innocent voyage to the Royal City."

"That's good to hear," said the White Whale, "for I hate pirates—or criminals of any sort, for that matter. Particularly the captain of this ship. Do you know, he's had it in for me for years? Look at that," he said, rolling his huge eye back.

All over the whale's body were harpoon shafts—dozens of them.

"Oh," cried Gremlin sympathetically, "that's awful!"

"I don't know why he's been picking on me all these years," sighed the leviathan. "There are other fish in the sea. I'm pretty phlegmatic by nature, but enough is enough. Those harpoons hurt. That's why I sank the ship."

"I can hardly blame you," Gremlin commiserated.

"Since you're not pirates," said the whale, "I'll be happy to give you a lift to the mainland on my back."

"Thank you," said Zeppelin, "that's white of you."

"Step lively, now," said the whale sharply. "I think she's about to go down. Oh, and watch that hole in the top of my head. Blow you fifty-feet high if you're not careful."

Soon the three of them were on their way, coasting smoothly through the sea. Zeppelin and Gremlin looked back just in time to see *Il Hombre Dangereux* disappear beneath the waves.

18. Homecoming

It wasn't very long before land was sighted.

"Can you swim?" asked the whale.

"No," admitted Zeppelin, "we're landlubbers."

"That's too bad," sighed the whale, "because I can't take you right into shore. I'm a mammal, but I'm hardly amphibious. Besides, I don't want to scare the bejeebers out of anyone swimming near the beach."

"That is a problem," said Gremlin.

"I've got it," the White Whale said. "Just up the coast there's a big cliff with an overhanging rock. You ought just to be able to climb safely from my back onto that."

This proved indeed to be true, and soon Zeppelin and Gremlin were standing atop the promontory, waving a fond farewell to their friend as he churned out to sea again.

"Keep straight ahead," he had counseled them. "It's clear sailing from here on in."

For the first time since they left home, the children found themselves unimperiled by their surroundings. They found a paved road winding through gently rolling hills, numerous helpful signs ("This way to the Royal City; 3 miles"), tidy little homes along the way, friendly villages, and jolly peasants who waved as they passed.

The only thing that marred their walk was that Zeppelin developed a blister from the leather strap on his sandal. He discarded the strap, but continued to limp.

"The thong is ended," Zeppelin complained, "but the malady lingers on."

They reached the Royal City without further incident. When they saw the metropolis, they could hardly believe their eyes. It enveloped, stunned, and overwhelmed them. They had to stop to gape at every skyscraper and theatre marquee.

But for all its size, the Royal City was strangely deserted. Zeppelin and Gremlin grew more and more puzzled as they looked into each empty shop window, restaurant, and pub. Finally they saw an old man sitting despondently on the curb with his head in his hands.

"Where is everybody?" Gremlin inquired.

"Oh, they're all down at the Imperial Palace overthrowing the king and queen," said the old man. "I'd be there too, but my asthma is bothering me today, and I don't want to get in a stuffy old crowd. Still, I'd like to be doing my bit to oust those rascals."

"Those rascals," said Gremlin haughtily, "happen to be my mommy and daddy."

They marched away, leaving the old man all astonied.

Pretty soon they came to the Royal Palace itself, where there was no doubt that an uprising really was taking place. Thousands of citizens milled around, yelling and carrying placards, most of them unimaginative ("Down with the King," "Down with the Queen," "Sick, Simpering Tyrannus") but some of them lengthy and ingenious ("It never reigns but what it pours" and *"Le roi le veut,* eh? Well, *nous ne voulons pas le roi!"*).

At the moment Gremlin and Zeppelin arrived, the predominant cry was "Storm the palace," and the mob seemed about to do just that.

"We have to stop this," cried Gremlin to her companion, "come on." And with these words the stalwart children pushed to the front of the crowd, where Gremlin raised an arm and shouted "Halt!"

Taken aback, the throng halted.

"Aren't you ashamed," Gremlin scolded them, "turning against your beloved sovereigns this way?"

"Beloved, balderdash," someone shouted.

Another yelled, "Who do you think you are, anyway, the Royal Princess?"

A cry of "Stone her! Stone her!" went up.

"Let him who is without sin," said Gremlin piously, "cast the first stone."

"Beloved, balderdash."

A red-headed man in the crowd, who happened to be without sin, immediately sidearmed a rock which missed Gremlin, but struck Zeppelin on the forehead and knocked him flat.

"As a matter of fact," Gremlin continued, "I *do* happen to be the Royal Princess, and I demand that you stop this appalling demonstration at once."

The mob began to hoot and jeer, until one woman at the front of the crowd, who had been studying Gremlin intently, raised her voice above the uproar and shouted "Stop!"

The crowd quieted.

"She really is the Royal Princess," said the woman. "Reason I can tell is . . ."

"I know," said Gremlin, "the mole on my right earlobe, the birthmark on my left elbow, and my blue-green eyes."

The temper of the crowd changed immediately at this news. Swept up by sentimental and patriotic emotions engendered by Gremlin's sudden and dramatic reappearance, they began to cheer wildly, cry, and hug one another. "The princess has returned," they shouted. "Our long lost white hope has come back to us."

"Go in peace now," Gremlin commanded them, "and don't let me catch you getting unruly again."

The crowd dispersed and went meekly back to their homes.

Zeppelin looked up, rubbing his bruised forehead. "What hit me?" he said.

"Just a rock," Gremlin told him as she helped him to his feet. "Now let's go in and introduce ourselves to my parents."

They knocked on the front door, to which was posted a notice announcing, "Rabble keep out."

"Can't you read, peasant?" a frightened voice from inside called. "Get away from here. We got enough trouble without revolutionaries."

"For your information," replied Gremlin sternly, "my name is Gremlin, princess of Etaoin and daughter to your employers. I demand that you open the door at once and that you give me your name, rank, and serial number."

"You've certainly caught on to your new position quickly," whispered Zeppelin admiringly.

The door was opened by a wizened, bent old man, who said, "I'm sorry I didn't recognize you through the closed door, your Highness, even though it has been only fourteen years since I saw you in your cradle. My name is Rhombus, and I am head manservant in the king's household. I hope you will not hold this regrettable lapse in efficiency against me."

"Where are my parents?" said Gremlin coldly.

"They are huddled in the throne room," Rhombus told her, "awaiting the onslaught of the mob."

"There will be no onslaught," said Gremlin. "Show me to them."

Rhombus led them to the king and queen, who recognized their daughter at once, of course. A lengthy sequence of tearful greetings followed, as Zeppelin stood by shuffling his feet in boyish embarrassment.

"So at last our little daughter is home again," said the king finally, blowing his nose. "But I fear, my child, that you have come at a perilous moment in our reign. The natives are restless."

"Never mind all that," said Gremlin confidently, "I'll take care of it. Now, I want you to meet my foster brother, Zeppelin, who has helped me arrive safe and sound through all my dangerous adventures. I hope you will make him feel at home here."

"He shall be as a son to us," the queen assured her.

"You children must be exhausted after your long journey," said the king. "I'll have Rhombus show you to your rooms."

"Oh," said Gremlin. "About Rhombus: after he's taken us to our rooms, I think you should reprimand him. He kept us waiting on the doorstep and called us rabble. I don't think much of that kind of treatment."

The king grew angry. "Rhombus, is this true?"

"Yes, your Majesty," replied the old man meekly, "I regret to say that it is."

"Then I have no recourse but to have your head cut off." The king turned to Gremlin. "I hope you consider that sufficient punishment."

"Oh, yes," Gremlin said. "That's capital."

19. The Palace of Art

In the next few years Gremlin grew into a beautiful and gracious young lady, loved and revered by her subjects.

While she had proved from her very first appearance at the capital city that she could be stern—indeed, even strict—her regal bearing and her kind concern for the people kept most Etaoinians content and respectful. She spent much of her time in beneficent activities—distributing box lunches to the poor, giving away bicycles to the most patriotic children of the community, sponsoring village dances and folk festivals, and a myriad other good works.

Zeppelin, who had been knighted by Gremail decree and set up luxuriously in court, reacted—it is sad to record—to his new environment in a different way. He took to wine, overeating, loose women, and staging fights between rabid aardvarks (a practice forbidden by law). All this, it was whispered at court, betrayed Zeppelin's peasant birth. "You can take the boy out of the country,"

. . . spent much of her time in beneficent activities.

sneered a viscount, "but you can't take the country out of the boy."

Worst of all, Zeppelin began to cast a puffy, envious eye on the throne.

One day Gremlin and Zeppelin were out in the royal carriage surveying thrones, principalities, and powers. As they jostled along a village lane not far from the imperial city, Gremlin ordered the driver to stop the vehicle.

"Why," asked Zeppelin, "did you order the driver to stop the vehicle?"

"Shhh," shhhed Gremlin, "listen!"

What they heard was a familiar voice from the past ringing out in clear melodious tones across the village square. They looked out the carriage window and, sure enough, there was their old acquaintance, the poet of the wood, standing on a soapbox addressing in verse an assembled crowd of four children and a dog:

"A wiseman of faculties fecund
Found a theory of truth when he reckoned
That when worst comes to worst
The last shall be first
And the next-to-the-last shall be second."

Zeppelin, recalling the poet's inertia when he and Gremlin were captured by the giant, suggested that she have him seized and punished.

"No," said Gremlin, who was never one to hold a grudge. "I think he may prove useful. Oh, poet," she called, "come here a moment."

The bard excused himself from his listeners and walked over.

"Do you remember us?" said Gremlin. "I'm the royal princess now, but ten years ago I was just a little girl, and while my ex-brother Zeppelin here and I were listening to you read your poetry in the forest we were seized by a giant named Umlaut and carried away."

"You really ought to avoid those run-on sentences, your Highness," scolded the poet. "Anyway, I'm glad you escaped."

"The reason I wanted to talk to you," said Gremlin, "is that I've been looking for a poet of the realm and wondered whether you'd like the job."

"Poet laureate, eh?" said the poet. "Well, I don't know that I approve of socialized art. But I accept. I shall not seek to know what my country can do for me but what I can do for my country."

"You're rationalizing," muttered Zeppelin, who was sulking because Gremlin wouldn't throw the poet in irons.

When the three of them arrived at the palace, Gremlin had her servants prepare a suite of rooms for the bard, complete with an ivory desk, dozens of gold pens, and reams of watermarked Corrasable bond paper.

Then Gremlin made everything official by having her sire softly strike the poet's shoulder with his sovereign scepter in a solemn ceremony, and say, "I appoint you poet of the realm."

"Thank you, your Majesty," replied the poet of the realm. "That I might try to justify my selection to this august position, I shall now go to my quarters and compose the official national anthem."

"That will be fine, my boy," yawned the king.

A half-hour later the bard burst into the dining room, where the royal family were having lunch, excitedly waving a piece of paper which he thrust onto the king's plate.

"I've finished it," cried the poet exuberantly, "complete with annotations. And though I say it who shouldn't, it's a terrific piece of work."

The king fished the paper out of his *pâté de foie gras* and found the following poem on it:

The Love Song of the Ancient Khayyam

the theme
becomes
apparent
to the
children
of Baal

We're not the best, but we're the last
Of prestidigitations past
(Generic term, you say—oh, no:
We are a magic lantern show
Of some amazement). Over there
Nasturtiums bloom around a bear

Performing handsprings on a tight
Rope, high above and out of sight.

the reader is warned of impending abstruseness

Enough of that. We are the best
Darned manikins that ever dressed
In cashmere and some other things
So hairy that a peasant sings
In childish awe and simple trust
(While fields erode and tractors rust).

ethnic transilience

I am the shadow, I his *frère*,
I am the muse of *mal de mer.*

back to puberty

Lately languished Lorelei;
On her navel lit a fly.
Lolly hollered, "Land o' Goshen,"
And leaped about with some commotion.

Jimmy Porter took the slops,
Hit his mother in the chops.
Sadly iterated Jimmy,
"Mother, you've become so phlegmy."

Mammon, Moloch, et al.

The burgeoning greengrocer, Sam,
Said to his mistress meek, "I am
A mart of all that I have, pet
(But deeper, deeper, into debt)."

I am the muse of mal de mer.

The maid said to the *mise-en-scène:*
"O, la, sir, you are off again."

the lyric impulse asserts itself in trochees

Boughs of willow, wispy met,
Embraced although their leaves were wet.
Said one, "Kindly do not foment
Me; it's not the proper moment."

The sloughs flow through the flues so slow.
Oh, no. Great growly Russians. Oh!

"You're fired," said the king upon completing the poem. He also extended his right thumb downward and made an abrupt, loud noise with his tongue.

"Aw, shoot, your Highness," said the poet. "It's a swell anthem."

"Hmmph," grunted the king. "'Idylls of the King,' 'King Dagobert and St. Eloi,' now, there's the kind of stuff I like. You sound like some sort of revolutionary."

"*Ars gratia artis,*" murmured the ex-poet of the realm as he slunk dejectedly out of the dining room.

20. The Song of Zeppelin

Unfortunately, the poet's hour at court, together with the king's last remark to him, had left him with some very strange ideas indeed. Directly he left the royal family the poet wandered into Zeppelin's quarters, where the dissolute duke was sitting on a chaise longue caressing a chambermaid and drinking a vodka martini.

"I just lost my job," the poet announced glumly.

"Good," said Zeppelin. "I never liked you anyway."

"That's a pity, because I had a proposition to make to you."

"I'm listening," said Zeppelin casually.

"I understand," said the bard, "that you have aspirations to the throne."

"Oh, yes," said Zeppelin. "I'm the great pretender."

"Then, come to the Enchanted Forest with me. With my eloquence and your influence we could organize all the witches and goblins and giants in the area and overthrow the government."

"Say, poet," said Zeppelin admiringly, "that is one great idea." He rubbed his hands together gleefully. "Of course," he added loyally, "it must be a bloodless coup. Not a hair of Gremlin's head must be harmed."

"Not a hair," the poet repeated sinisterly.

They left that night for the Enchanted Forest, plotting and scheming as they went along, and arrived early the next week. The first creature they attempted to recruit was the bear, who listened to their first few words of entreaty and promptly ate them both.

For little did the luckless duo know that the bear was a highly placed civil servant, the chief, in fact, of the local branch of CIO (Counter-Insurgency Organization), with a license to eat traitors. One of the traitors, he noticed, tasted curiously familiar.

So the bear, after taking a well-earned and pleasant nap, dutifully filled out a report of the incident in triplicate and mailed it to the palace. One copy, as was customary, found its way across Gremlin's desk.

The Princess' heart sank as she read it, for the description of one victim was exactly that of the lately vanished Zeppelin. And Gremlin knew that she must save her childhood companion, even if it meant using the last of her precious three wishes, which she had been reserving for a great universal cause like world peace or additional major league jousting franchises.

"Not a hair."

Thus did Gremlin, guarded by twelve of Etaoin's finest, set out for the Enchanted Forest to interrogate the bear, who, alas, confirmed her darkest suspicions.

In less time than it took Gremlin to say "Mafficking Malachi," her fairy godmother appeared before her.

"Hiya, honey," said she. "My, how you've grown! Now, small talk aside, what can I do you for this one last time?"

"I'm afraid," said Gremlin, "that you'll have to rescue my ex-brother again."

"You choose to jest!" exclaimed the fairy godmother. "I swear, that's the most calamity-ridden boy I've ever seen." She spotted the bear. "Good grief! Isn't that the same bear I rescued him from before?"

The bear nodded.

"It takes all kinds," said the fairy godmother. "Well, here goes."

Thrice she waved her magic wand in a circle and there stood Zeppelin, abashed and tearful. The fairy godmother gazed on him severely.

"Before I go," she said, "I just want to tell you you ought to be ashamed of yourself."

"You certainly ought," echoed the hungry and patriotic bear.

"Now," said the fairy godmother, "it's off to that great shell game in the sky."

"G'by, fairy godmother," said Gremlin. "You've been super."

"Grem," said Zeppelin when she had gone, "I know I can never undo the wrong I've done you. But I promise that from this day forward, henceforth and forevermore, I shall devote myself to a life of chastity, humility, and true religion."

The penitent and regenerate young man proved to be as good as his oath. Immediately afterward, Zeppelin went into spiritual retreat with the noted mystic and recluse, F. Stanley F. X. Cruet, who gave him intensive instruction in theology and ecclesiastical history. Following this, Zeppelin took holy orders and soon became one of Etaoin's best-loved clerics, as well as Gremlin's own spiritual counselor.

And at the spot where Zeppelin's wondrous conversion took place, a miracle occurred. Overnight an artesian well appeared, flowing with enough ice-cold grape Kool-Aid for any and all who would partake. A grateful and pious citizenry erected a chapel at the spot, and thereafter referred reverently to Zeppelin as *Zeppelin à Bucket,* which, roughly translated, means "Zeppelin has the bucket."

21. The Secret Admirer

As Gremlin grew into lovely maturity, her parents naturally decided that it was time she choose a suitable mate, in anticipation of the day when she would assume the mantle and duties of Queen of the Realm. And so a variety of suitors—domestic and imported, of new and ancient vintage—began appearing at Court. Gremlin looked them all over, but found none to her liking.

"Here's a nice-looking boy," her mother would say.

"He's Trojan," Gremlin would complain, "and *trop jeune.*" (And that was the last time she saw Paris, who, as it turned out, was not to be trusted around women anyway.)

Like all young girls, what Gremlin was looking for was love. And the idea of a pre-arranged marriage did seem an awfully unlikely way to go about it. But Gremlin dutifully decided to look around for a while longer, then settle for the best of the courtly, handsome, well-scrubbed, dull lot.

But love came to Gremlin, as it does to many a young girl, in a strange and wonderful and unexpected way. One day her maidservant brought her the daily mail, which contained, as usual, a voluminous stack of fan letters, crank requests, and Chamber of Commerce brochures. Being a good princess, Gremlin had never hired a private secretary or any servant of that sort, and faithfully read each letter that came to her. On this occasion she was rewarded with a singularly moving and simple missive:

"Dear Princus:

> i can not rite so good but i seen yore pitcher on a fotograffy wich was in our noospaper here. boy you sur are butiful. i hav fall in luv with you. i am a little cripple-up feller. i aint but 3 an a haf feet tal. that is wy i cant revel my tru idennity to you, becauz of im so ugly. another reson i cant is becauz of my countri an yourn are mortel ennemis. but if you wood rite me a leter i wood be as happy as a grig. i cant tel you my name, lik i say, but if you wood sen it to the gnome king, Shrdlu, i wil get it ok. luv and kises.
>
> an admier"

Now, who, Gremlin wondered, could this secret admirer be? Whoever he was, Gremlin lost no time in replying to his love-smitten epistle.

Dear kind friend, (she wrote)

I was touched and honored by your sincere and heartfelt letter (you will excuse what may be a redundancy).

The only thing that disturbed me is this: You repeatedly downgraded yourself about your looks, height, etc. I need only remind you that a man is as big as he thinks he is and that furthermore beauty is in the eye of the beholder, and skin-deep to boot.

As for your obviously warm affection for yours truly: While it would be immodest of me to offer any sort of overt encouragement, I would like to say that, while I admire your humility, faint heart, on the other hand, ne'er won fair lady (you will excuse my self-flattery), that I should be happy to hear from you again, that, after a suitably lengthy correspondence, an actual meeting would not be out of the question, and that I should certainly like to know your name.

Yours truly,
Gremlin
Princess of Etaoin

A lengthy and passionate correspondence did indeed follow, although Gremlin's bashful admirer would never reveal his name. But after receiving the twenty-seventh or twenty-eighth of these love letters, Gremlin was certain of one thing: she was in love.

22. The *Fin de Siècle*

One dark day, as Gremlin was waiting for the mail, the king and queen summoned her to appear before them in the throne room.

"My child," said the queen, "your father and I feel that you have vacillated long enough in selecting a mate. So we have chosen one for you."

"Please, Mother," cried Gremlin. "I'd rather do it myself."

"You are to be married," said the king firmly, "to Pepe ffofington. Lord ffofington's boy."

"He's a nice lad," her mother said kindly. "You'll like him. Nine years old, and just as cute and playful as he can be."

"Isn't that terribly young?" said Gremlin. "I'm twice nine."

"He's young," the queen admitted, "but he's daily growing."

"It's all arranged," said the king. "Wednesday next you will be joined in holy wedlock to ffofington. Before that, of course, there will be a gala fête."

"For me," moaned the heartbroken girl, "it will be a fête worse than death."

"Never mind," said the king sternly. "You are to look upon it as a fête *accompli.*"

Gremlin went back to her room and fell down on her big featherbed and cried and cried and cried. When she had recovered somewhat, she wrote a letter to her admirer in Shrdlu, urgently begging him to reveal himself and come to her rescue lest a terrible calamity befall her.

Then, fearful of entrusting so important a message to the mails, Gremlin sent for Zeppelin, and, after explaining her dilemma, dispatched him to Shrdlu to deliver the note in person.

"Grem," said the gallant padre, "I shall not fail you now."

Day after day rolled by, however, without a single word from either faithful minion or mysterious lover. Through bridal shower, gown fitting, and rehearsal, the anxious girl watched, and waited. In no time at all the fateful nuptial day itself had dawned.

At the height of the morning's prothalamial festivities, as the young bridegroom entertained the guests by practicing thugee rope tricks on the servants, Gremlin was quietly handed a telegram by her chambermaid. Her heart leapt with joy as she read it:

"I shall not fail you now."

Dere princus: (it said)

> boy you sur wil be surprise to here who i am i bet, an i never wood have tole you nether only they gone make you mari that punk kid sos all i can do is cum over ther an tak over yore kingdum stop i can do that you see on account of im the gnome king of Shrdlu, name of Grig, an powerfull as al getout stop then mabe you an me can mak butiful musick together huh stop
>
> luv an kisses
>
> Grig

Sure enough, a greasy horde of Shrdluans—with the estimable Zeppelin and the intrepid Grig at the vanguard—was at that moment besieging the palace, which was soon overtaken.

In the aftermath, the king and queen and several dozen obstreperous ffofingtons were beheaded.

Gremlin and the gnome king were married at once by Zeppelin (now Archbishop). They joined Etaoin-Shrdlu to form the Holy Roman Empire, and ruled it wisely and well for many years.